This book belongs to . . .

This edition published in 2017 by

Albury Children's Books
Albury Court, Albury, Thame, Oxfordshire, OX9 2LP
United Kingdom

For orders: Kuperard Publishers and Distributors
office@kuperard.co.uk | 020 8446 2440

A CIP record for this title is available from the British Library.

ISBN Paperback: 978-1-910571-66-8
ISBN Hardback: 978-1-910571-67-5

Printed and bound in Turkey

Princess
Bum Bubble

Catherine
Vāse

Albury Children's

The King and Queen were very proud of their daughter, Princess Gwendolina. She was the cleverest, the most beautiful, the most princessy princess anyone had ever seen. She was perfect in every single way. Well, almost perfect.

There was just one teeny, weeny thing . . .

Princess Gwendolina
broke wind.
royal ball

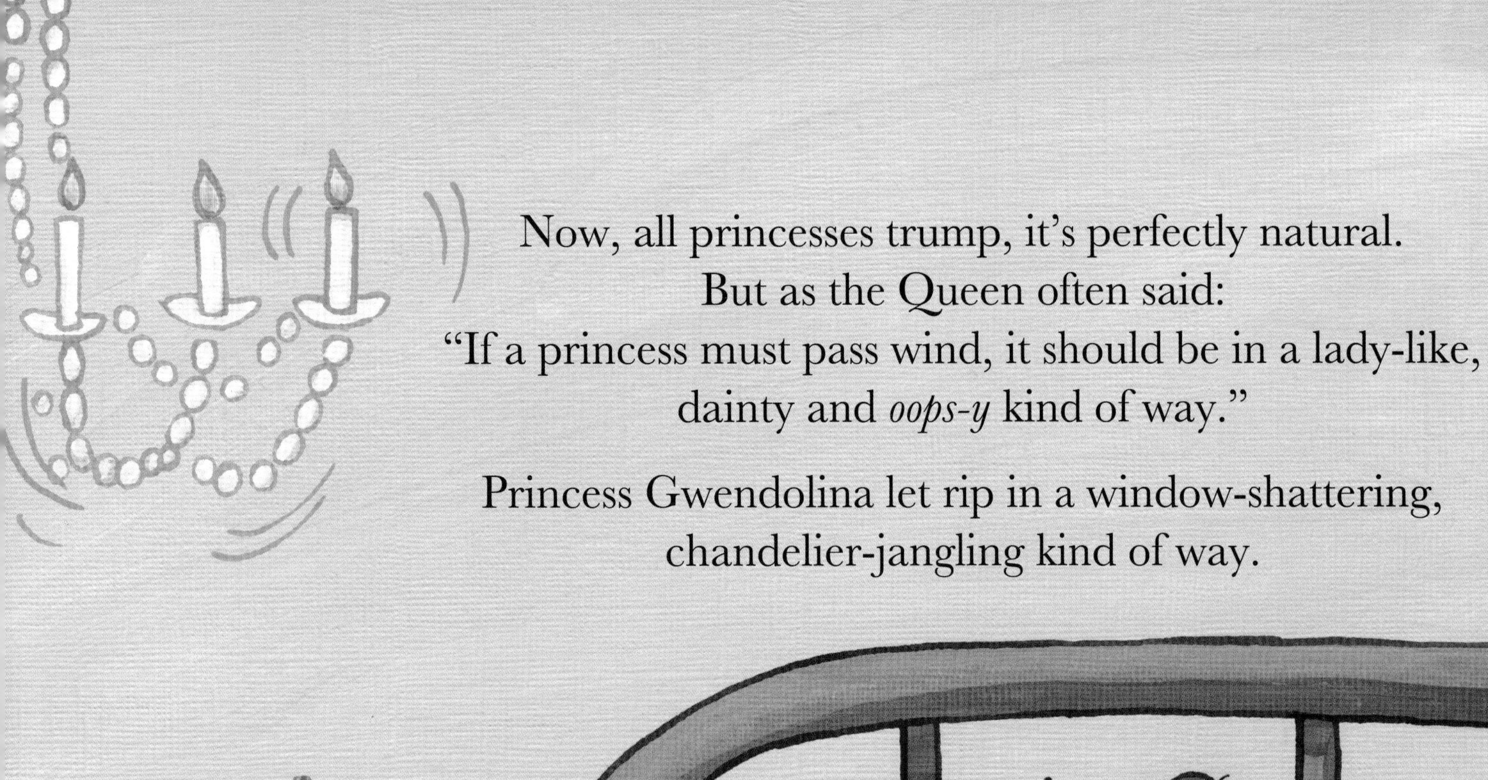

Now, all princesses trump, it's perfectly natural.
But as the Queen often said:
"If a princess must pass wind, it should be in a lady-like, dainty and *oops-y* kind of way."

Princess Gwendolina let rip in a window-shattering, chandelier-jangling kind of way.

Gwendolina let out cheek squeaks at tea.
"More cake, Grandma?"

PARP!

She got botty burps on important occasions.
"I now declare," said Gwendolina—

PARP!

She got bum bubbles at sporting events.
"Congratulations," said Gwendolina—

PARP!

"We have to DO something!"
said the Queen to her husband,
"or no one will want to
marry her!"

So a new regime was declared.

“No more beans!”

decreed the King.

“We’ll blame the dog!”

proclaimed the Queen.

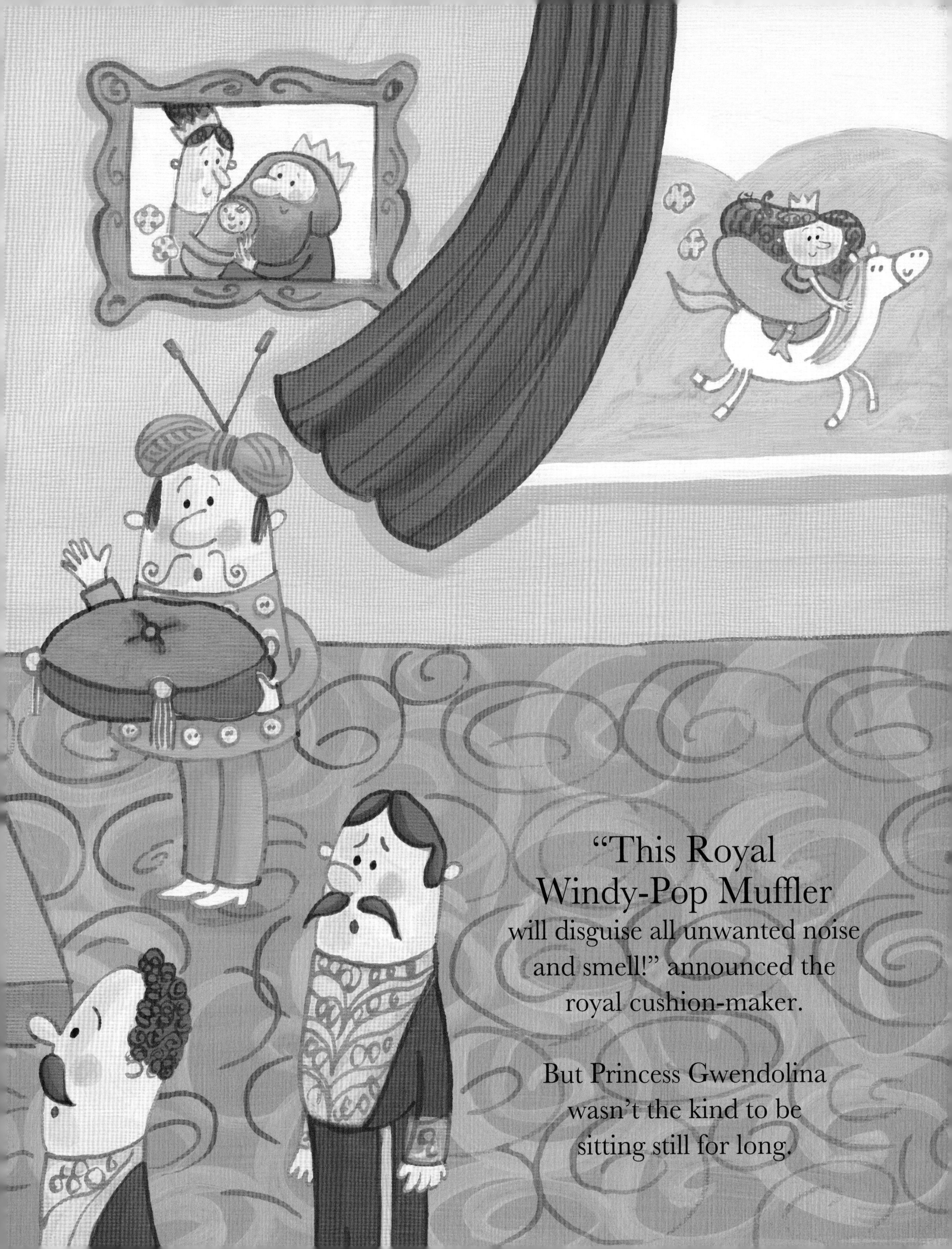

"This Royal
Windy-Pop Muffler
will disguise all unwanted noise
and smell!" announced the
royal cushion-maker.

But Princess Gwendolina
wasn't the kind to be
sitting still for long.

Meanwhile in a land far, far away

(well, just around the corner) lived a handsome prince, Prince Norbert.

Prince Norbert was bored with the attention he was getting from all the dainty, lady-like girls who desperately wanted to marry him. So he decided to go for a ride.

"Good afternoon!" said Prince Norbert.
"Good day to you!" said the Queen.

PARP! went Gwendolina.

"Sorry, good sir," said the Queen,
"... that was the dog!"

"You noisy hound!"
cried the King.
"You pongy pup!"
said the Queen.

What an odd couple,
thought Prince Norbert,
but who is that dazzling beauty?!

He asked the King
and Queen if he could
**take the Princess
out on a date.**

"Erm," said the Queen,
rather surprised. "Of course."
"But we'll come too," said the King.

And he whispered to the Queen:
"I'll blow this trumpet to hide the parps!"
"And these roses will disguise the smell,"
the Queen whispered back.

So Prince Norbert and
Princess Gwendolina
went out on their date.

The date was a wonderful success.

As the weeks went by, they went everywhere together. Prince Norbert loved having the company of this beautiful princess, who was

clever and kind . . .

and funny too.

But there was one teeny, weeny thing on his mind . . .

"Your Majesties," he declared to the King and Queen, "I have met so many princesses, but none compares to your daughter. Princess Gwendolina is
so *different*—"

The King and Queen looked at each other anxiously.

"I would like . . .

to marry her!"

"But – but –" the Queen stammered loudly, ***"she…"***

"Breaks wind!" said the Prince. "Yes, she lets one go every now and then, but hey, nobody's perfect."

The Queen blushed as red as a rose.
The King put away his trumpet.

"Princess Gwendolina,"

said Prince Norbert . . .

"Will you marry me?"

"Erm," said
Princess Gwendolina thoughtfully . . .

“No, thanks.”

“Oh!” said the Prince.
“What’s wrong with me?!”

"Nothing!" replied the Princess.
"I simply have more important things to do…

"But you can come with me!"

Other books by Catherine Vāse

The Big Hair Affair

Lawrence is the best hairdresser in the jungle.
He's a whizz with the scissors, a pro with the comb – and he's good at listening too. But jealous Marvin can't understand why Lawrence is so popular, and when Lawrence gets a letter inviting him to do the hair of a Very Famous Giraffe, Marvin is determined to ruin his big day . . .

I Love You Mummy. . .
I Love You Daddy!

If Mummy were a sound, what would she be?
The gentle purr of a cat!

But what would Mummy be if she were a place, a fruit or a bird? Find out, then flip the book over to find out what Daddy would be if he were a toy, a meal or a noise!

"A delightful celebration of love"
MUMSENSE